This book belongs to:

....

....

....

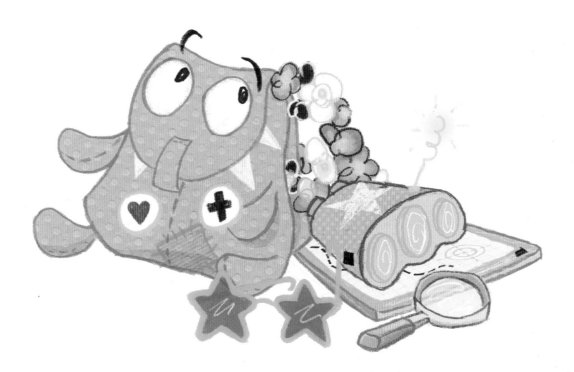

To Angelina
and Samantha – JC

For Seren – LS

SKY PRIVATE EYE AND THE CASE OF THE MISSING GRANDMA
First published in Great Britain in 2017 by Five Quills
93 Oakwood Court, London W14 8JZ
www.fivequills.co.uk
Five Quills is a trademark of Five Quills

Edited by Natascha Biebow at Blue Elephant Storyshaping
Designed by Ness Wood

A CIP record for this title is available from the British Library

ISBN 978 0 9935537 0 7

1 3 5 7 9 10 8 6 4 2

Printed in China

SKY PRIVATE EYE
AND THE CASE OF THE
MISSING GRANDMA

Jane Clarke   Loretta Schauer

FIVE
QUILLS

In Fairytale Town, Sky Private Eye was mixing up a special order of her Just-in-Case Cupcakes when . . .

beep beep-beep!

The red cherry on the Cupcake Communicator began to flash.

"It's a fairytale emergency!" Sky gasped.

She wiped her sticky hands, took a deep breath and answered, **"Sky Private Eye. Can I help?"**

"Granny's gone missing!"
wailed Little Red Riding Hood.
"The Big Bad Wolf must
have kidnapped her
or . . . or gobbled
her up!"

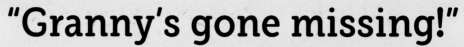

"Clues and rescues are our
speciality," Sky said, reassuringly.
"And cupcakes of course.
Keep calm, we're coming to help!"

Sky grabbed her detective backpack and hopped on her scooter. "Our mission is a grandma rescue!" she told Snuffle. And with a

yum,yum, yum, vrum, vrum vrum!

they whizzed off.

The Map Nav led them down a narrow leafy lane, round Big Rock, over Babbling Brook and past the Old Oak to Granny's house.

Little Red Riding Hood dashed out. "I'm so worried!" she gasped.

"Keep calm," said Sky, gently. "Have a cupcake while we look for clues . . ."

Sky Private Eye searched Granny's bedroom. "Granny's bed hasn't been slept in," she said. "Her summer clothes are missing . . . and look! A travel brochure."

"Granny hasn't been eaten by the Big Bad Wolf –
she's gone on holiday!"

Fairytale

BEACH

SHOP

Suddenly, Sky heard a howl at the
front door. She rushed to investigate.

Snuffle was snuffling at a long, shaggy hair caught on a rosebush.

It was a grey **wolf hair!** Sky put it in an evidence bag.

"**Quick!**" Sky shouted.
"The Big Bad Wolf was here!
I think he followed Granny.
Jump on the scooter, everyone!"

It was very busy at Fairytale Beach.
Sky took out the TriOculars.

As she watched, the Big Bad Wolf looked hungrily at Granny. He opened his jaws . . .

"Uh-oh . . ." Sky gasped. "He's going to eat Granny!"

But Granny reached into her hamper and held out a hotdog.

SNAP!
The Big Bad Wolf

gobbled it up.

"PHEW! We need to spy on them to find out what's going on,"
Sky said. "We'll go undercover. Here, put on these disguises!"

Sky, Little Red Riding Hood and Snuffle
crept up on Granny and the Big Bad Wolf.

They shadowed them
along the beach,

they tailed them
through the waves,

they snuck up
on them at the
Ice Queen Parlour.

The Big Bad Wolf looked very hungry.
A big gob of drool plopped down his chin . . .

"Break cover!" yelled Sky.

"How lovely to see you!" Granny cried.
"Have you met Wolfie?"
"Wolfie?" spluttered Little Red Riding Hood.
"That's the Big Bad Wolf. He wants to
gobble you up!"

Sky held up the evidence.
"He was at your cottage,"
she said. "Snuffle found proof."
"I . . . I might have gone there to take a
little nibble out of Granny . . ."
Wolfie confessed.

"But we've been having so much fun on holiday, you've forgotten all about eating me, haven't you?" said Granny.

"Oh no, I haven't!" the Big Bad Wolf growled, and he made a lunge for Granny . . .

"This is a sticky situation!" cried Sky, pulling out her apron and throwing it over the wolf's head. In a blink of an eye, Sky and Snuffle had the suspect all wrapped up.

Sky threw off her disguise. "It's time to **Bake it Better!**"

She got out her Carrycake Kit and began to bake cupcakes as fast as she could. She'd just popped them into her on-the-go-oven when . . .

Little Red Riding Hood gasped, **"The wolf's escaping!"**

"Lunchtime!"
snarled the Big Bad Wolf.

"Stop!"

Sky wedged her
Stir Crazy spoon into
the Big Bad Wolf's mouth.

Ping! went the
on-the-go oven.
Sky pressed the
Quick Cool
button, and just as
the Big Bad Wolf
spat out the spoon . . .

. . . she shoved a **Just-in-Time** Cupcake between his fangs!

Little Red Riding Hood, Granny, Snuffle and Sky looked at one another nervously. Was the special recipe right?

Wolfie gobbled up the cupcake and rolled over
to have his tummy tickled.
"Aw! Wolfie's so cute!" Granny exclaimed.

YUM! YUM!

Sky clapped her hands. "Now that you've eaten one of my special cupcakes, you'll never want to gobble anyone ever again. You and Granny can be friends!"

The next time Little Red Riding Hood went to visit Granny

there was no Big Bad Wolf, just a big, friendly one.

"Mission accomplished!"
said Sky Private Eye.
"Woof!" Snuffle agreed,
and when Sky wasn't
looking, he licked out
the mixing bowl.

Sky's Vanilla Cupcakes

Makes 12 wolf-print cupcakes. Eat one to prevent Granny-gobbling.

INGREDIENTS

140g sweet dreams caster sugar
120g plain flour from Fairytale Mill*
1 1/4 teaspoons baking powder
Pinch of fairy story salt
40g unsalted butter, softened
120ml whole milk from the Cow Who Jumped
Over the Moon.*
1 egg from Chicken Licken*
1/4 teaspoon of vanilla essence

Shop-bought ingredients will also work.

For the frosting:
80g unsalted butter
250g icing sugar
25 ml milk
1/4 teaspoon of vanilla extract
Chocolate drops and buttons
Magic sprinkles

To make the cupcakes:

1. Ask your grown-up to preheat the oven to 170°C (HOT!)
2. Put on your Bake it Better apron and measure out the ingredients.
3. In a large mixing bowl, use your Stir Crazy spoon to beat together the sugar, flour, baking powder, salt and butter. Stop when the mixture looks like the sand on Fairytale Beach.
4. Slowly pour in half of the milk (60ml), and stir it in.
5. In a separate bowl, whisk the egg, vanilla essence and the rest of the milk.
6. Pour the egg mixture into the flour mixture. Beat until it is as silky as Snuffle's ear.
7. Place the cupcake cases on a baking tin and fill each 2/3 full with the cupcake mixture.
8. Ask your grown-up to put them in the oven. Bake for 20-25 minutes, (HOT!) until the tops look golden or your grown-up sticks in a toothpick and it comes out clean.
9. Ask your grown-up to put the cupcakes out of reach of (HOT!) hungry wolves and let them cool while you make the frosting.

To make the frosting:

10. Beat the butter and icing sugar together, then slowly add the milk and vanilla extract. Keep beating until the mixture looks like fluffy white clouds.

11. Ice the cupcakes and decorate with chocolate paw prints and magic sprinkles.

(HOT!) *You will need an adult to help.*